Shells used for brown dye

WALNUTS

CARDING COMBS

Branches used for brown dye

JUNIPER

STORE-BOUGHT DYES

THE WEAVER

DYE BUCKET

For pushing strands of woven yarn together

COMB

Flowers used for yellow dye

RABBIT BRUSH

To tighten yarn while weaving

PIN

Roots used for yellow dye. Twigs, leaves & berries used in black dye

SUMAC

To sew rug ends into tassels

SACKING NEEDLE

GLENMAE'S RUG

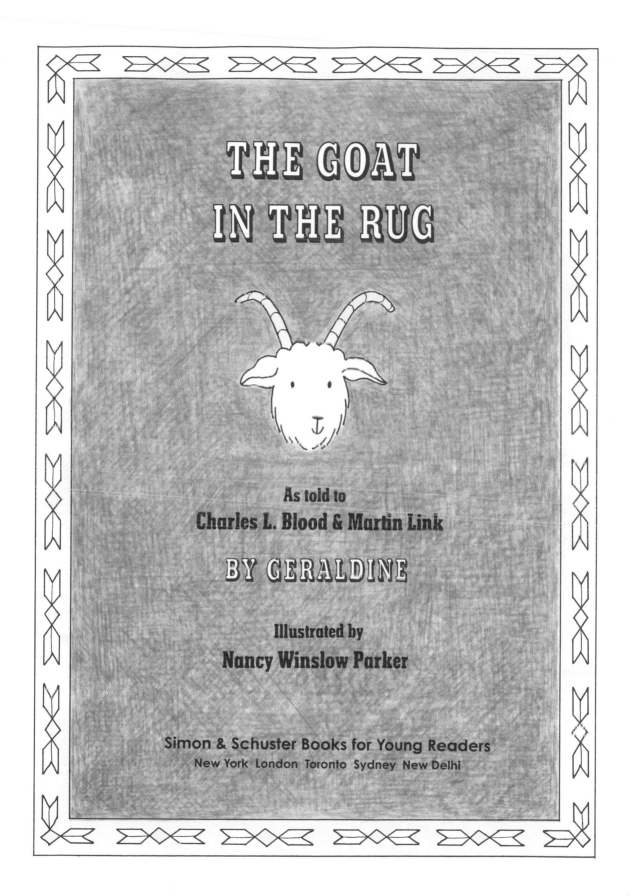

THE GOAT
IN THE RUG

As told to
Charles L. Blood & Martin Link

BY GERALDINE

Illustrated by
Nancy Winslow Parker

Simon & Schuster Books for Young Readers
New York London Toronto Sydney New Delhi

Simon & Schuster Books for Young Readers
Simon & Schuster
1230 Avenue of the Americas
New York, NY 10020
Manufactured in China

10 9 8 7 6 5

Library of Congress Cataloging in Publication Data

Blood, Charles L. (date).
  The goat in the rug.

  Originally published by Parents' Magazine Press, New York.
  SUMMARY: Geraldine, a goat, describes each step as she and
her Navajo friend make a rug, from the hair clipping and
carding to the dyeing and actual weaving.

  (1. Navaho Indians—Textile industry and fabrics—Fiction. 2.
Rugs—Fiction. 3. Hand weaving—Fiction. 4. Indians of North
America—Textile industry and fabrics—Fiction) I. Link, Martin A.,
joint author. II. Parker, Nancy Winslow.
III. Title.
(PZ.B6227Go 1980)   (E)   80-17315
ISBN 978-0-02-710920-7

0912 SCP

For Glee 'Nasbah,
The Navajo Weaver

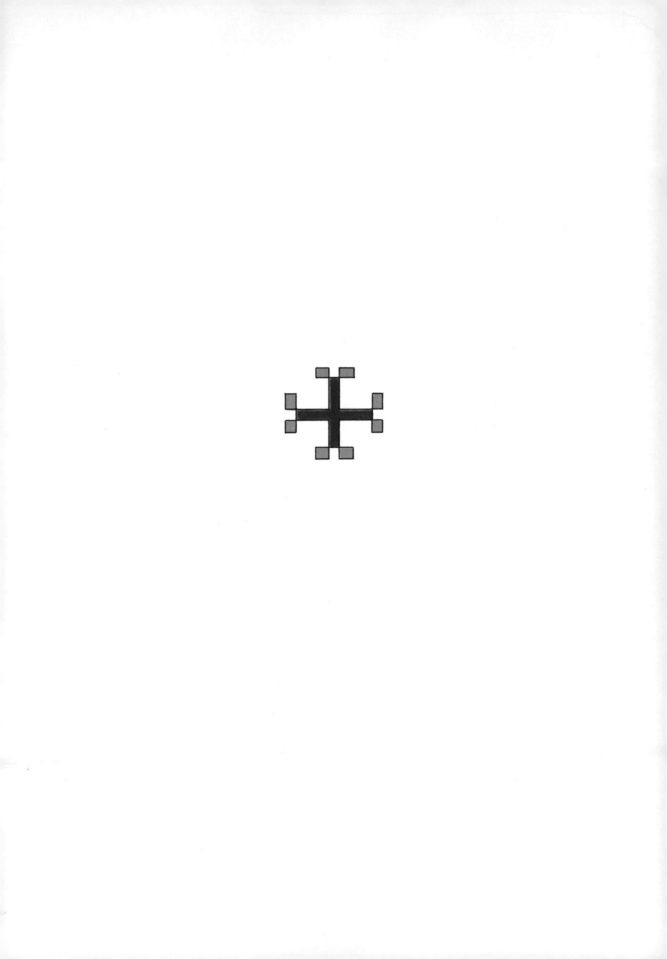

My name is Geraldine and I live near a place called Window Rock with my Navajo friend, Clen mae. It's called Window Rock because it has a big round hole in it that looks like a window open to the sky.

Glenmae is called Glenmae most of the time because it's easier to say than her Indian name: Glee 'Nasbah. In English that means something like female warrior, but she's really a Navajo weaver. I guess that's why, one day, she decided to weave me into a rug.

I remember it was a warm, sunny afternoon. Glen-mae had spent most of the morning sharpening a large pair of scissors. I had no idea what she was going to use them for, but it didn't take me long to find out.

Before I knew what was happening, I was on the ground and Glenmae was clipping off my wool in great long strands. (It's called mohair, really.) It didn't hurt at all, but I admit I kicked up my heels some. I'm very ticklish for a goat.

I might have looked a little naked and silly after-wards, but my, did I feel nice and cool! So I decided to stick around and see what would happen next.

The first thing Glenmae did was chop up roots from a yucca plant. The roots made a soapy, rich lather when she mixed them with water.

She washed my wool in the suds until it was clean and white.

After that, a little bit of me (you might say) was hung up in the sun to dry. When my wool was dry, Glenmae took out two large square combs with many teeth.

By combing my wool between these carding combs, as they're called, she removed any bits of twigs or burrs and straightened out the fibers. She told me it helped make a smoother yarn for spinning.

Then, Glenmae carefully started to spin my wool—one small bundle at a time—into yarn. I was beginning to find out it takes a long while to make a Navajo rug.

Again and again, Glenmae twisted and pulled, twisted and pulled the wool. Then she spun it around a long, thin stick she called a spindle. As she twisted and pulled and spun, the finer, stronger and smoother the yarn became.

rabbitbrush
wild onion
cliffrose
sumac
juniper
walnuts
dock

A few days later, Glenmae and I went for a walk. She said we were going to find some special plants she would use to make dye.

I didn't know what "dye" meant, but it sounded like a picnic to me. I do love to eat plants. That's what got me into trouble.

While Glenmae was out looking for more plants, I ate every one she had already collected in her bucket. Delicious!

The next day, Glenmae made me stay home while she walked miles to a store. She said the dye she could buy wasn't the same as the kind she makes from plants, but since I'd made such a pig of myself, it would have to do.

I was really worried that she would still be angry with me when she got back. She wasn't, though, and pretty soon she had three big potfuls of dye boiling over a fire.

Then I saw what Glenmae had meant by dyeing. She dipped my white wool into one pot...and it turned pink! She dipped it in again. It turned a darker pink! By the time she'd finished dipping it in and out and hung it up to dry, it was a beautiful deep red.

After that, she dyed some of my wool brown, and some of it black. I couldn't help wondering if those plants I'd eaten would turn all of me the same colors.

While I was worrying about that, Glenmae started to make our rug. She took a ball of yarn and wrapped it around and around two poles. I lost count when she'd reached three hundred wraps. I guess I was too busy thinking about what it would be like to be the only red, white, black and brown goat at Window Rock.

It wasn't long before Glenmae had finished wrapping. Then she hung the poles with the yarn on a big wooden frame. It looked like a picture frame made of logs—she called it a "loom."

After a whole week of getting ready to weave, Glenmae started. She began weaving at the bottom of the loom. Then, one strand of yarn at a time, our rug started growing toward the top.

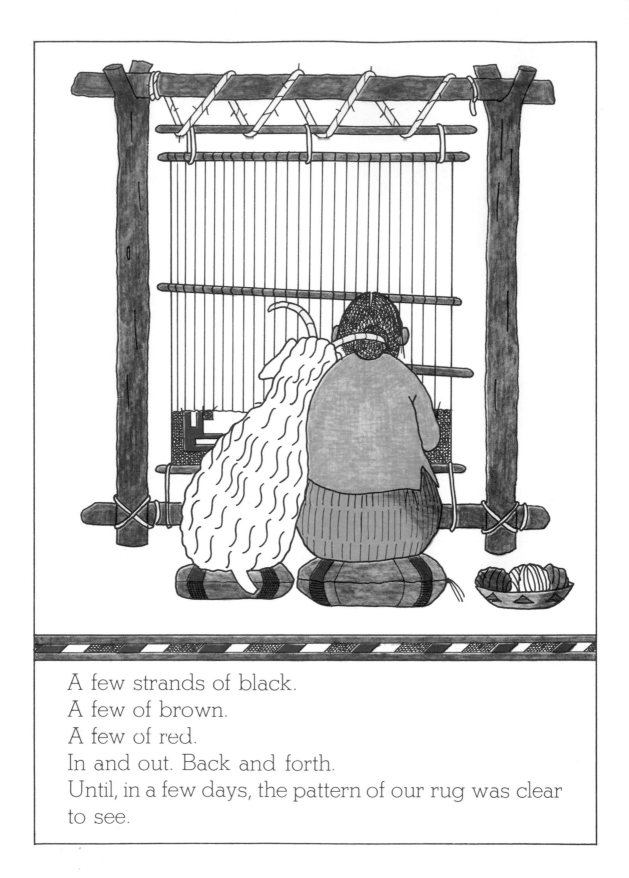

A few strands of black.
A few of brown.
A few of red.
In and out. Back and forth.
Until, in a few days, the pattern of our rug was clear
to see.

Our rug grew very slowly. Just as every Navajo weaver before her had done for hundreds and hundreds of years, Glenmae formed a design that would never be duplicated.

Then, at last, the weaving was finished! But not until I'd checked it quite thoroughly in front...

. . . and in back, did I let Glenmae take our rug off the loom.

There was a lot of me in that rug. I wanted it to be perfect. And it was.

Since then, my wool has grown almost long enough for Glenmae and me to make another rug. I hope we do very soon. Because, you see, there aren't too many weavers like Glenmae left among the Navajos.

And there's only one goat like me, Geraldine.

This is the true
story of a weaver
and her goat
who lived in the
Navajo Nation at
Window Rock,
Arizona.

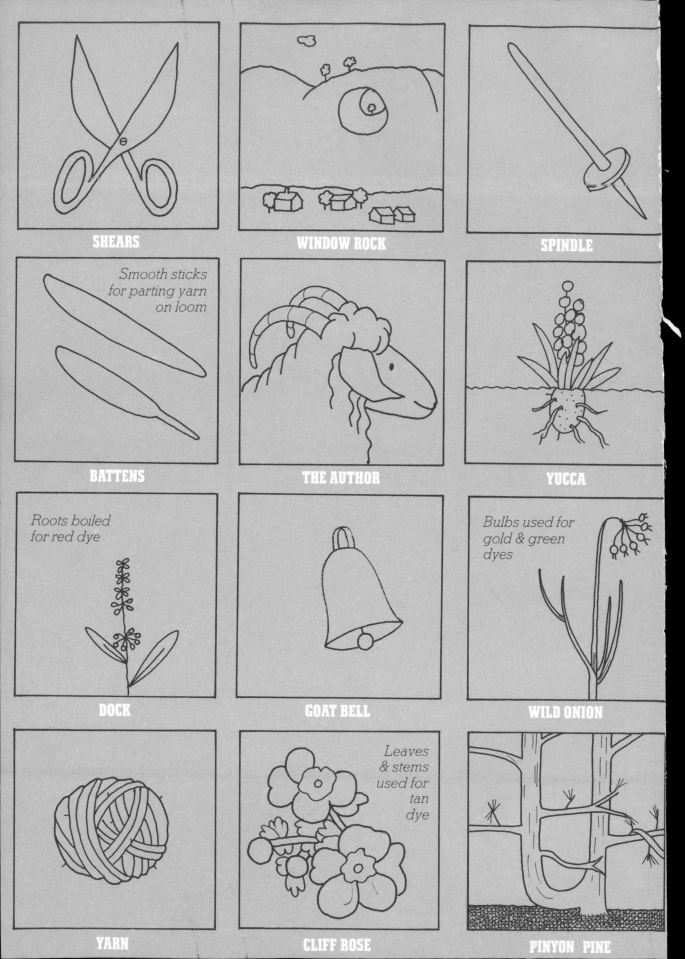

SHEARS

WINDOW ROCK

SPINDLE

Smooth sticks for parting yarn on loom

BATTENS

THE AUTHOR

YUCCA

Roots boiled for red dye

DOCK

GOAT BELL

Bulbs used for gold & green dyes

WILD ONION

YARN

Leaves & stems used for tan dye

CLIFF ROSE

PINYON PINE